IT COULD BE WORSE

Einat Tsarfati

translated by Annette Appel

WALKER BOOKS
AND SUBSIDIARIES

LONDON · BOSTON · SYDNEY · AUCKLAND

Albertini and George floated side by side on what was left of their ship.

Albertini was feeling discouraged. George, on the other hand, was playing his harmonica cheerfully.

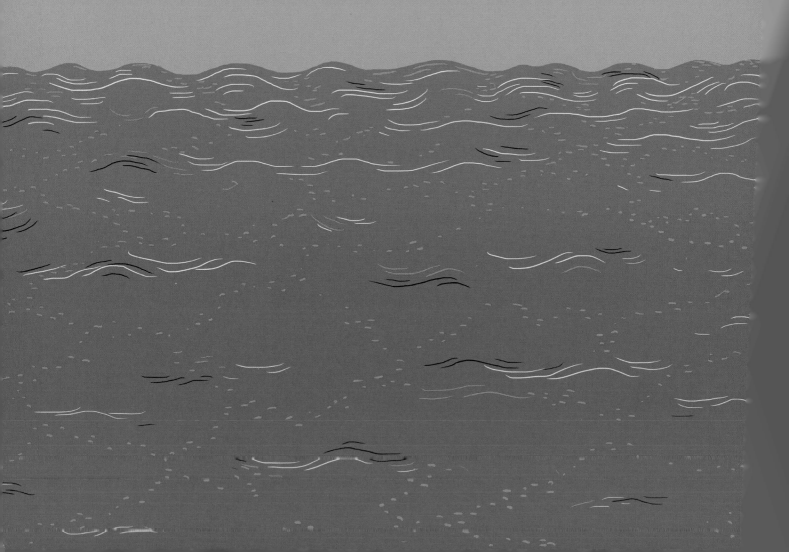

Then it started to rain.

"This is so unfair!" shouted Albertini.

"It could be worse . . ." said George.

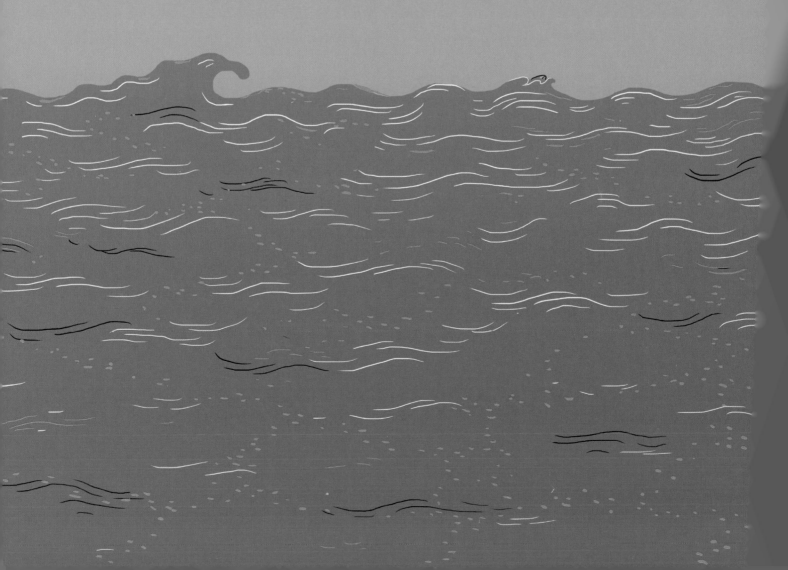

And as he said it, a school of flying fish flew above their heads.
And not just flying fish, but flying fish with diarrhoea.

"ARGHHH!" said Albertini.

But George just laughed. "It could be much worse . . ."

George had barely finished his sentence when out of the sea rose six mermaids singing the sort of song that gets in your head and won't leave for a week.

"This is really bad!" said Albertini. He couldn't help humming the mermaids' infernal tune.

"It could be worse," said George, singing along.

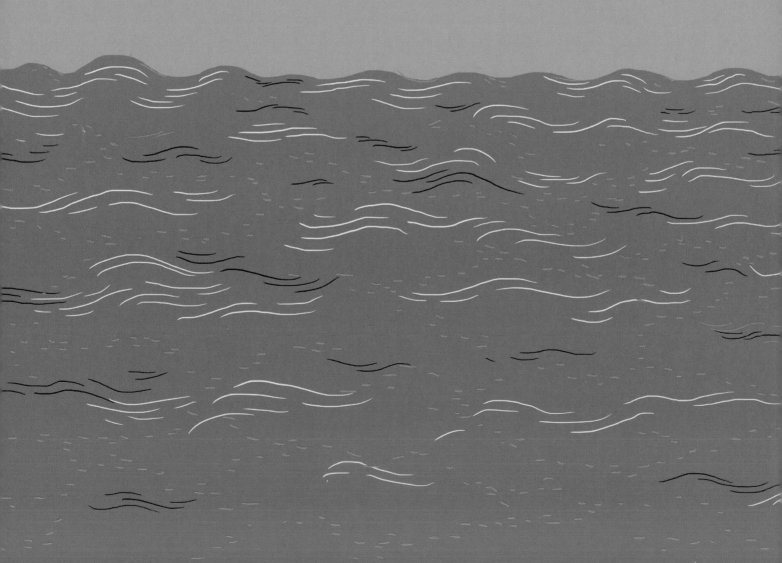

And then, out of nowhere, a ghost ship full of pirates appeared.

"AHₕHH!" cried Albertini.

George was busy playing the mermaids' song on his harmonica, but he paused to say, "It could be worse."

"Oh, like maybe a ghost ship full of pirates on a moonless night?" shouted Albertini. He was really worked up now.

And of course George replied, "It could be worse."

And of course, just then,
an ark full of animals approached.

An ark full of animals who hadn't eaten for forty days! They howled
and roared and licked their lips at the sight of the two sailors.

And now Albertini was certain. It could *not* be worse than this . . .

until a gigantic sea anemone pulled
the two friends down to the bottom of the sea.

"It COULOLOLOLD BLEE WORSSSSE," said George as a bloom of jellyfish floated around them.

And then!

"I think this whale has eaten only
tuna sandwiches for a month,"
said Albertini, holding his nose.

"I love tuna," said George.
"It could be much, much worse!"

The two friends landed on an island covered in smelly seaweed.

"This stinks," said Albertini. "Plus, I am hungry."

And you already know what George said . . .

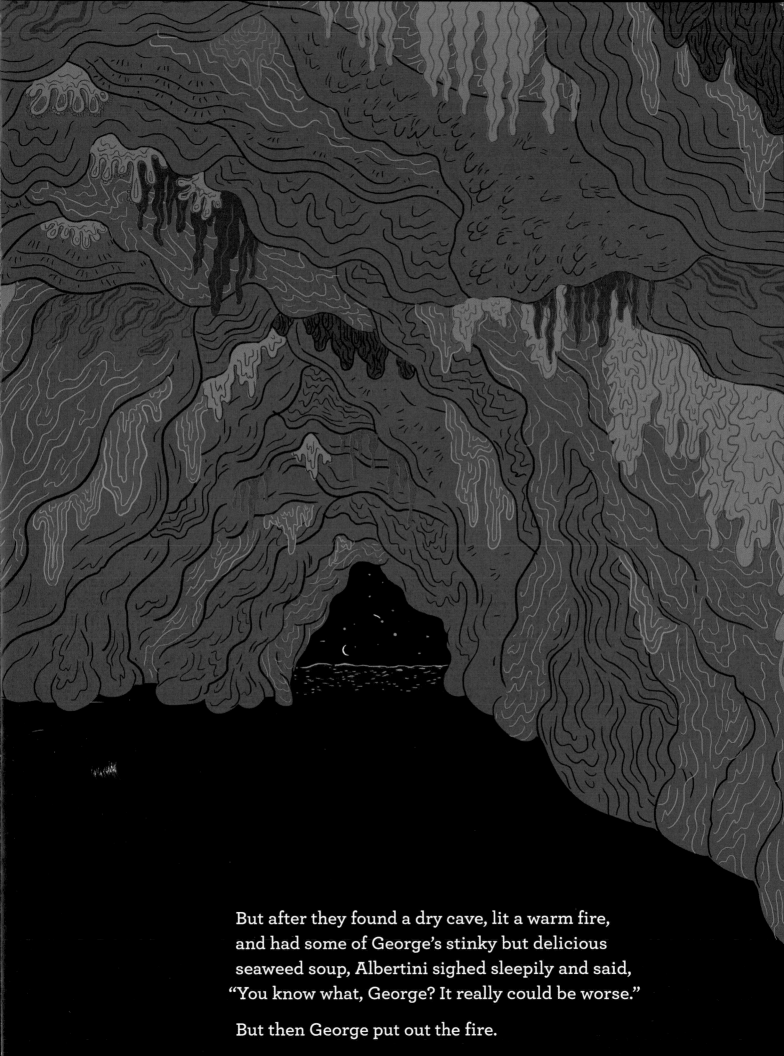

But after they found a dry cave, lit a warm fire,
and had some of George's stinky but delicious
seaweed soup, Albertini sighed sleepily and said,
"You know what, George? It really could be worse."

But then George put out the fire.

"ARGGHHH!"

the two friends shouted together.

"This does look bad," George admitted at last.

But then Albertini managed to get the fire started again.

"I can't believe it!" he cried. "It's our crew!"

"George! Albertini! You won't believe what a night we had!" shouted their captain to his two lost sailors.

"Oh," said Albertini with a smile, "trust me – it could have been much, much worse."

And together they all sailed off towards a new day.

First published 2021 by Walker Books Ltd
87 Vauxhall Walk, London SE11 5HJ

10 9 8 7 6 5 4 3 2 1

© 2021 Einat Tsarfati

Translated from Hebrew by Annette Appel

The right of Einat Tsarfati to be identified as the author-illustrator of this work has
been asserted by her in accordance with the Copyright, Designs and Patents Act 1988

This book has been typeset in Archer

Printed in China

British Library Cataloguing in Publication Data: a catalogue record for this book is
available from the British Library

ISBN 978-1-5295-0244-2

www.walker.co.uk